A Giant First-Start Reader

This easy reader contains only 50 different words,
repeated often to help the young reader develop
word recognition and interest in reading.

Basic word list for *The Goofy Ghost*

a	good	on
all	goofy	one
and	hall	rug
are	haunted	spooky
at	he	still
bad	hiss	thanks
bang	hisses	that
be	house	the
big	in	they
boo	is	to
boos	little	too
but	littlest	tries
comes	live	trips
crash	night	try
does	not	want
ghost	nothing	wants
ghosts		what

The Goofy Ghost

Written by Sharon Peters

Illustrated by Tom Garcia

Troll Associates

Library of Congress Cataloging in Publication Data

Peters, Sharon.
  The goofy ghost.

    Summary: A young ghost learns to be spooky.
    [1. Ghost stories] I. Garcia, Tom. II. Title.
  PZ7.P44183Go   [E]   81-2573
  ISBN 0-89375-533-8 (lib. bdg.)   AACR2
  ISBN 0-89375-534-6 (pbk.)

The little ghosts live in a haunted house.

They are good and spooky.

They hiss and they boo.

But the littlest ghost is not spooky.

He is goofy.

Crash! Bang! What is that?

The littlest ghost trips on the rug.

He trips in the hall.

The littlest ghost trips on nothing
at all!

"Try to hiss. Try to boo."

"Try to be spooky—not goofy!"

The littlest ghost tries and tries.

But he is still goofy.

One night, a big, bad ghost comes.

He wants to live in the haunted house.

The good little ghosts try to be spooky.

They hiss and they boo.

But the big, bad ghost is spooky, too.

He hisses and he boos, too.

The littlest ghost tries to be spooky.

He tries to hiss and boo, too.

But he is still goofy.

Crash! He trips on the rug.

Bang! He trips in the hall.

What is that? *That* is spooky!

The big, bad ghost does not want to
live in the haunted house.

Thanks to the littlest ghost.

Thanks to the goofy ghost!